Kare

**Other books by
Ann M. Martin**

P. S. Longer Letter Later
(written with Paula Danziger)
Leo the Magnificat
Rachel Parker, Kindergarten Show-off
Eleven Kids, One Summer
Ma and Pa Dracula
Yours Turly, Shirley
Ten Kids, No Pets
With You and Without You
Me and Katie (the Pest)
Stage Fright
Inside Out
Bummer Summer

For older readers:

Missing Since Monday
Just a Summer Romance
Slam Book

THE BABY-SITTERS CLUB series
THE BABY-SITTERS CLUB mysteries
THE KIDS IN MS. COLMAN'S CLASS series
BABY-SITTERS LITTLE SISTER series
(see inside book covers for a complete listing)

Little Sister

Karen's Copycat
Ann M. Martin

Illustrations by Susan Crocca Tang

A
LITTLE APPLE
PAPERBACK

SCHOLASTIC INC.
New York Toronto London Auckland Sydney
Mexico City New Delhi Hong Kong

ISBN 0-590-50059-7

12 11 10 9 8 7 6 5 4 3 2 1   9/9 0 1 2 3/0

Printed in the U.S.A.   40
First Scholastic printing, March 1999

*The author gratefully acknowledges
Gabrielle Charbonnet
for her help
with this book.*

Karen's Copycat

The Best Kids Ever

"Rain, rain, go away, come again another day," I sang.

"Andrew Brewer wants to play," chimed in my little brother, Andrew. (He is four going on five.)

We looked out the window. The rain had not gone away. It was still a windy, rainy March morning.

"Well, we can always play inside, Andrew," I said.

"I do not really want to play," replied Andrew. "I just sang that because it went with the song. I want to sit here and wait for Merry."

I nodded. All I wanted to do was wait for Merry too.

Oh, I have not told you who Merry is. I have not even told you who I am yet!

My name is Karen Brewer. I am seven years old. I have blonde hair and blue eyes and freckles. I live in Stoneybrook, Connecticut. I am in second grade. I have *two* families. And I will tell you more about myself in a minute.

But first I have to tell you about Merry Perkins. Because Mommy was starting a new job, Andrew and I needed someone to look after us during the day. We needed a nanny to arrive before school started and stay until Mommy came home in the afternoon. Andrew and I helped choose the nanny ourselves.

We chose Merry. This was going to be her first day with us. She would be arriving any minute to help us get ready for school.

I was sure that Merry would be the perfect nanny for us — just like Mary Poppins! Their names even sound alike.

Andrew and I sat and waited patiently for Merry. I hummed a little. Andrew hummed a little. I kicked my heels against the side of the couch. Andrew kicked his heels against the side of the couch.

I was going crazy. And I could tell that Andrew was going crazy too.

"Mommy!" I called. "When will she get here?"

Mommy came out of the kitchen. "She should be here any minute," she said. Mommy sat on the couch with us. (She did not kick it with her heels.)

"You two seem pretty excited about your new nanny," said Mommy.

"Oh, yes," I said. "I am very excited. Merry is great! We are going to have so much fun with her."

"I am glad you are looking forward to spending time with her," said Mommy. "But you know, it might take you some time to get used to having Merry around."

"What do you mean?" I asked.

"Well, we all like Merry," said Mommy. "Still, she is new to you, and you will be new to her. You will have to get used to each other."

What was there to get used to? Merry was wonderful, and I was . . . well, I was pretty wonderful too, when you got right down to it. And so was Andrew. How could there be any problems?

"Everything will be fine," I told Mommy. I patted her shoulder. "I am sure of it."

"Okay, Karen," said Mommy. "I am glad you think so."

"I do," I said.

Mommy smiled at me, and then she headed back to the kitchen.

After Mommy left, I thought for a moment. (I am always thinking. It is very tiring sometimes.) I was sure that I liked Merry. I was sure that Andrew liked Merry. And I was sure that Merry liked us too. If she did not, she would not have accepted the job as our nanny. But what if Mommy was right?

What if we had trouble getting used to Merry? What if she had trouble getting used to us? We needed to make sure everything went smoothly.

"Andrew, I know how we can make sure that Merry is really happy being our nanny," I said.

"How?" Andrew asked.

"We can be on our *best behavior*. We can try to be the best kids Merry has ever nannied. Merry will fall in love with us. And we will all be happy."

"That is a great idea, Karen," said Andrew.

"Thank you," I said politely. I was already on my best behavior!

Karen Two-Two and Andrew Two-Two

Now I need to tell you about my two families. So here I go.

A long, long time ago, when I was little, Mommy and Daddy and Andrew and I lived together in Daddy's big house. But Mommy and Daddy decided they did not love each other anymore and they got divorced. So Mommy moved into her own little house. Andrew and I went with her.

Daddy stayed in the big house, where he had grown up.

After awhile Mommy met a nice man named Seth Engle. They got married, and Seth came to live in the little house. He is our stepfather now. Seth brought his dog, Midgie, and his cat, Rocky, with him. Mommy, Seth, Andrew, Midgie, Rocky, Emily Junior (my pet rat), Bob (Andrew's hermit crab), and I all live together at the little house.

Daddy also got remarried, to a gigundoly nice woman named Elizabeth Thomas. She is our stepmother. Elizabeth already had four children of her own, and they all came to live with her in Daddy's big house. Elizabeth's kids are Sam and Charlie, who are practically grown-ups (they are in high school); Kristy, who is thirteen and who is the best stepsister ever; and David Michael, who is seven, like me, but who goes to a different school.

After Daddy and Elizabeth got married, they adopted my little sister from a faraway country called Vietnam. Emily Michelle is two and a half. I love her so much that I named my pet rat after her.

There are so many people at the big house (so many pets too) that Elizabeth's mother, Nannie, came to live there and help take care of everyone. (It is important to remember that my big-house Nannie is not my little-house nanny. *Nannie* is short for "grandmother." I do not know what *nanny* is short for.)

Now Andrew and I go back and forth between the little house, where Mommy lives, and the big house, where Daddy lives. We spend a month at one house, then a month at the other house.

Even though Emily Junior and Bob travel back and forth with us, most of our stuff does not. That is because we have two of a lot of things — one for each house. I have two sets of clothes, two collections of books, and two stuffed cats named Moosie and Goosie. Plus I have two houses and two families, two mommies and two daddies, and two pieces of Tickly, my special blanket.

I also have two best friends. Hannie Papadakis lives across the street and one house down from the big house. Nancy Dawes lives next door to the little house. We call ourselves the Three Musketeers. Our motto is "All for one and one for all!"

Because Andrew and I have two of so many things, I started calling us Andrew Two-Two and Karen Two-Two. (I got the idea from a book called *Jacob Two-Two Meets the Hooded Fang*.)

Hey! I just thought of something! Now I even have two "nannies" — Nannie, my stepgrandmother, and Merry, my nanny.

And speaking of Merry, the doorbell finally rang! I smoothed my hair and put a big smile on my face. Andrew did the same. We ran to the door. We were on our best behavior. And we were ready to greet Merry on her very first day of work.

Copycat Andrew

"Merry!" I shouted as I flung open the door.

"Karen! Andrew!" said Merry. "Good morning! How nice to see you!" She shook out her umbrella. "Still in your pajamas? Run upstairs and get dressed. We do not want to be late for school." Merry's smile was even bigger than mine.

Andrew and I dashed upstairs to put our clothes on.

While we were dressing, Mommy said

good-bye to us. She had to go to her job making jewelry at the crafts center.

We rushed downstairs as soon as we were dressed. Merry had fixed our breakfast. I sat down at my place. There was a bowl of oatmeal with raisins and brown sugar on top. The raisins made a smiley face, with brown-sugar hair. My juice glass had a wedge of orange stuck on the rim. My paper napkin was folded into a sort of flower shape.

Everything looked gigundoly fancy and special.

"Wow!" I said. "This is bee-yoo-ti-ful!"

Andrew looked at me. "Yes!" he said quickly. "Bee-yoo-ti-ful! Thank you."

Merry was wonderful. And this was just her first hour! I was glad Andrew and I were planning to be wonderful too.

Usually I love school, but today I wanted to spend all my time with Merry. As soon as the bus pulled up to my stop at the end of the day, I leaped off, said good-bye to Nancy, and raced home.

I found Merry and Andrew in the kitchen, working on an art project. (I love art projects!)

Merry had taken out a stack of old *National Geographic*s. She and Andrew were looking through them and cutting out pictures of fish and other sea life. They were pasting the pictures onto a blue sheet of construction paper. The blue looked like water.

"Would you like to help us with our aquarium collage, Karen?" Merry asked.

I could see that the aquarium collage was almost done.

"Would it be okay if I started a new collage?" I asked politely. "Maybe I will make a farm."

"That is a great idea, Karen," said Merry.

I flipped through the magazines and ate my snack (peanut butter on rice crackers). Pretty soon I had cut out a good collection of animals, tractors, and other farm things. I started pasting them onto a fresh sheet of green construction paper. The green looked like fields.

Across the table from me, Andrew was looking at my farm scene.

"May I make a farm too?" asked Andrew nicely.

"Our aquarium is not quite filled up yet," said Merry. "We have a few more fish to paste down, plus this handsome crab."

She held up a picture of a crab. It was green and blue.

"I think I'd like to make a farm now," said Andrew.

"Well, okay, we can make a farm collage," said Merry. "Let's find some farm pictures." (I could make my collage on my own, but Andrew needed Merry's help with the scissors.)

I watched them flip through magazines for awhile. I had already cut out all the best farm pictures. All they could find were some teeny, tiny faraway cows and a building that did not look much like a barn. Andrew was upset. I did not want him to be upset in front of Merry. We were supposed to be on our best behavior.

"Here, Andrew," I said. I handed him my pile of farm pictures. "You may have these."

"Why, Karen," Merry exclaimed. "That is so nice of you, to share your pictures. What a good big sister you are."

I smiled. Merry was beginning to see how wonderful I was.

"I will work on a food collage instead," I said grandly.

"That will be fun, Karen," said Merry. "You are full of good ideas today."

I beamed. Merry was pleased with me already. Soon I was cutting out pictures of hot dogs, ice-cream cones, a roasting turkey, a pile of some weird beans, and lots of other foods. I started pasting them down.

I glanced up. Andrew was watching me. He was not working on his farm collage.

"I want to do foods," he said.

I raised my eyebrows. "What did you say?" I asked him.

"Foods," he said. "I want to make a food collage too."

I could not believe it. Andrew was copy-ing me.

"Andrew," I said, frowning. "You said you wanted to make a farm, and so I gave you — "

"I have an idea," said Merry cheerfully. "I think we should put away the collages for now, and listen to some music instead."

She started sweeping up the magazines, glue sticks, and construction paper.

I wanted to tell Andrew he was a copycat. But I decided I better not. Not in front of Merry. I did not want her to think I was dis-agreeable, or that Andrew and I bickered a lot. We usually do not.

"May I help you pick out music?" I asked.

"Yes, indeed," said Merry, walking into the living room.

Before I followed her, I frowned hard at Andrew.

Karen's Brilliant Idea

I soon stopped feeling mad at Andrew. We both knew it was important to stay on our absolute best behavior. We even shook on it.

The next afternoon Merry had another fun activity planned for us. We went to a crafts fair at the Stoneybrook Community Center.

"Some of my old students have some pieces in the fair," Merry said.

Besides being our nanny, Merry is a potter. She makes things such as mugs and bowls out of clay and sells them.

18

"That bowl is beautiful," I said, pointing to one of the pieces. It was green, with a red rim.

"It was made by one of my students," said Merry proudly.

"Are you going to have time to teach pottery, now that you are our nanny?" I asked.

"Yes. During the months that you two are at the big house, I will teach a children's pottery class," said Merry. "But during little-house months, I will be too busy taking care of you to teach a class. I am looking forward to having a little variety in my schedule. The only problem is . . ." Merry's voice trailed off.

"What?" I asked. "What is the problem?"

"Well, the nanny job came on rather suddenly," Merry said. "I had already agreed to teach a pottery class during March. So just this month, starting next Thursday, I will be teaching a class on Tuesday and Thursday afternoons."

"What will happen to us?" Andrew asked. His eyes grew big.

"That is the problem," said Merry. "Your parents and I have been looking for a baby-sitter who can take care of you on Tuesdays and Thursdays for the rest of the month. But we have not been able to find anyone so far. If we cannot find someone fast, I do not know what we are going to do."

I walked up and down the hall, looking at the crafts. I saw picture frames made of seashells. I saw handmade teddy bears and dried-flower arrangements and bird paintings. And lots of cups, plates, saucers, and bowls made out of pottery.

The pottery was really neat, I thought. I had never thought about pottery before. I was sure Merry would be pleased if I showed an interest in it. Someday maybe I could even take her class. . . . That was it!

"Merry!" I cried. I ran to her. She and Andrew were looking at a display of fancy leather belts. "I have the answer to your problem!"

"You do? And what is it?" Merry asked.

"The solution is that Andrew and I will

take your pottery class. I would love to take a pottery class." I was proud of my solution.

"Me too!" Andrew chimed in.

I beamed at Merry. I waited for her to say, "Karen, that is a stroke of genius."

Instead she said, "Karen, I am afraid you and Andrew cannot take my class."

"Why not?" I asked.

"Why not?" Andrew echoed.

"It is for older children. Eight- to eleven-year-olds."

"I am almost eight," I pointed out. "Because I am already seven. And Andrew is very mature for his age."

Andrew stood up tall.

Merry smiled. "I do not know, Karen. I am not sure it is a good idea. But there may not be any better options. I will talk to Seth and your mommy about it."

Yippee! Andrew and I high-fived. We were going to take pottery lessons. I was sure of it.

Merry Says Yes!

"Mommy, please!" I begged. "Pretty please. Pretty please with a cherry on top!"

Mommy smiled. "You certainly know how to ask nicely, Karen," she said.

It was later that afternoon. Mommy had come home from her job making jewelry. I had told her how Andrew and I could take Merry's pottery class.

Now Mommy, Merry, Andrew, and I were in the living room. We were talking about my brilliant idea.

Mommy did not seem convinced.

"Andrew and I want to learn how to make pottery," I pointed out. "Right, Andrew?"

"Yes," said Andrew. "I want to be in the class with Karen."

"I am happy that you are both so interested in pottery all of a sudden," said Mommy. "But the problem is, the class is for older children."

"We will act older," I promised. "We will pay attention. We will not misbehave. I will use my indoor voice. I am sure we will be no trouble at all."

"Well . . ." said Mommy. "It is true, it would be very convenient for me if you were to take Merry's class. I have not been able to find any other arrangement for you."

She was about to give in. I could tell.

"I suppose it is okay with me . . ." Mommy began.

I started to shout, "Hip, hip, hoo — " when Mommy cut me off.

"It is really up to Merry, however," said Mommy. "She is the teacher. It is her class. She has the final say."

Mommy turned to Merry. "What do you think, Merry? Will it be okay for Karen and Andrew to sit in on your class?"

"Oh, Merry, please," I said. "Pretty please with a cherry on top. Pretty please with a cherry and chocolate sprinkles on top!"

Merry laughed. "No chopped nuts?"

"Pretty please with everything on top," I said.

"That is quite a pretty please, Karen," said Merry. "Still, I am not sure. Will you and Andrew be able to keep up with the class? I do not want the other students to have to hold back."

"I am sure that we can keep up," I said. "I have made lots of things out of Play-Doh. That is almost the same as clay. And Andrew is an expert at making mud pies."

Merry smiled. "And will you both behave in class?" she asked.

"Oh, yes," I said. "I promise. Scout's honor." (I am not a scout, but if I were, I would have a lot of honor.)

"I promise too," said Andrew.

"Hmmm . . ." Merry said.

What more could I do? I had asked pretty please. I had pointed out all of our qualifications. I had promised scout's honor.

So Merry should have said yes by now. What was the problem?

Finally Merry said, "Okay. I guess it will be okay — *as long as Karen and Andrew promise to be on their best behavior.*"

Merry really stressed that last part, about the best behavior. It was almost as if she doubted whether we would behave. And we had already behaved perfectly for days.

"I promise!" said Andrew. He was jumping up and down. "We are going to take Merry's class, Karen!"

I did not jump up and down.

Merry had said, "I guess it will be okay." She had not said, "It will be fabulous if you take my class." Or "There is no one I would want more to take my class."

Instead she had hinted that we might cause trouble. That the other students would not like us. That we would hold others up.

And I had already promised to behave. I did not like having to promise again. But if I was going to take Merry's class, I knew I would have to.

"I promise to be on my best behavior," I said quietly.

"Great," said Mommy. "That settles it. Karen and Andrew will take the class. Thank you, Merry, for making an exception. It really gets me out of a tight spot."

I had gotten what I wanted. I should have been happy. But I was not. My feelings were hurt.

Maybe Mommy had been right when she said that we would have to get used to Merry.

The Three Musketeers

"It will be so much fun!" I said. I was telling Hannie and Nancy about Merry's pottery class. I had decided that what really mattered was that Merry had let Andrew and me into her class. I was sure that as soon as class started, Merry would see that she had made a good decision. In fact, she would like us even more, because we would be the best-behaved kids in the class.

"We are going to learn to use glazes, and how pots are fired, and — " I went on.

"That sounds so neat," said Hannie. "Maybe I could take the class too. I took pottery at summer camp. I am sure Mommy would let me if I asked."

"Me too," said Nancy. "I will ask my mommy. It would be great if the Three Musketeers could take the class together."

"The class is really for older kids," I explained. "Merry is making an exception for Andrew and me." I said "exception" in an important-sounding voice. I did not say that Merry was letting us in because Mommy could not find us another sitter.

"Oh," said Hannie, looking disappointed.

"Oh," said Nancy. "You do not think Merry could make an exception for us too?"

My friends seemed sad. I did not want to let them down. After all, if Merry thought I could handle the class, maybe she would think my friends could handle it also. I would ask her.

"Maybe I can do something," I said. "I bet it will be no problem to get you in the class."

"Great!" said Hannie.

"Super!" said Nancy.

"Absolutely not," said Merry.

"But — but — but, Merry," I stammered. "I sort of promised Hannie and Nancy that they could take your class too."

"I am sorry, Karen," said Merry. "It is out of the question. The class is for eight- to eleven-year-olds. You and Andrew are a special case. I am afraid I cannot allow any more younger children to attend."

"But — but — " I sputtered.

Merry waited for me to finish. I could not think of anything else to say. I thought about trying to look very, very sad. But I had a feeling that that would not work with Merry. (Actually, it does not work with Mommy, Seth, Daddy, or Elizabeth either.)

At last Merry said, "I wish I could help you out, Karen, but I just cannot. You will have to tell Hannie and Nancy that they cannot take the pottery class."

She did not seem angry with me. But she

did not look like she was about to change her mind either.

Boo and bullfrogs!

I could not understand why Merry could not make an exception for my friends too. If Merry really liked me, she would do it.

Maybe Merry did not like me so much after all. And she would not like me any better now.

I called Nancy first.

"Nancy," I said, "I have some good news and some bad news. Which do you want first?"

"The bad news," she said.

"Okay." I braced myself. "The bad news is that you and Hannie cannot take the pottery class."

"Oh, no!" Nancy cried. "Why not?"

"Merry said you are too young."

"But you are taking it," Nancy argued. "Even Andrew is taking it. He is only four."

"Four going on five," I pointed out.

"Whatever," said Nancy. I could tell she was angry. "What is the good news?"

"Actually, there is no good news," I said. "I only said that to make you feel better."

"Well, it did not work." Nancy hung up.

The call to Hannie was just the same. Except I left out the part about the good news. I felt bad that my best friends felt bad.

But I felt even worse about something else. I was still not sure whether Merry liked me. She seemed to. She was always nice to me. And I liked her a lot, even though she had not let Hannie and Nancy into her class.

But I still did not understand why Merry had not let the two Musketeers take the pottery class. If she *really* liked me, she would have.

The Perfect Potter

Hannie and Nancy were mad at me for a couple of days, even though I apologized to them. By Thursday, the day of my first pottery lesson, we were all friends again.

After school Merry drove Andrew and me to the community center. We arrived half an hour before the class was supposed to begin. Merry needed the time to set up the classroom.

"May I help?" I asked her. I was still on my best behavior.

"Thank you, Karen," said Merry. "You

may help me arrange the chairs around the tables. Each table gets four chairs."

I smiled at Merry and headed for the wall where the classroom chairs were lined up. Andrew followed me. I grabbed a chair and started to drag it toward a table.

I had already vowed to be on my best behavior for Merry. But maybe that had not been enough. I decided to go one step further. I would also be the best pottery student Merry had ever had. I would be the perfect potter. Merry would have to like me then, since pottery is one of her favorite things.

I pushed the chair under a table. I turned to get another and ran straight into Andrew, who was right behind me.

"Oops!" I said. "Why are you following me, Andrew?"

"I am not following you." He pushed his chair under a table, then raced back to the wall. "I want to help too," he said. He grabbed a chair and started dragging.

"Fine," I replied. "Just do not get in my way."

I was a little tired of Andrew. He had been following me everywhere lately. It seemed like I could not take three steps without tripping over him.

Pretty soon the other students began to arrive. They sat at the tables.

I scanned the classroom. Two girls were sitting at one of the tables. They were both older than me. They looked nice. I decided to sit with them.

Andrew followed me to the table and sat next to me.

"Welcome, students," said Merry when everyone was seated. "My name is Merry Perkins. I am your pottery instructor."

Merry asked the students to stand and introduce themselves. We did. (I said my name especially loudly. I like introducing myself.)

Then Merry walked around the room and put a large cube of clay in front of each student.

"Today I would like for us to get to know

the clay," said Merry. She picked up a cube like the ones she had given us. "Knead your clay. Work it between your fingers. Notice how soft it is, how heavy."

I picked up my clay and mashed it in my fingers. It was cool and heavy and wet. It was a little gritty. It felt good.

While we got to know our clay, Merry explained how the class would work. We would practice making several things. But most of them would not be fired. ("Fired" means baked in a hot oven called a kiln.)

Our beginner projects would not be thrown away, though. Unfired clay — even if it is all dried out — was never thrown away. We would put it into a recycling tub. That is a big container full of clay and water. As long as a project had not been fired, it could go in the recycling tub. There it would melt down into the water, become regular gooey clay again, and be reused.

By the third or fourth class, Merry explained, we would work on projects that would get fired. After firing, the projects would be glazed and refired. A glaze is like paint that hardens in the kiln.

Merry was an excellent explainer. Everything was very clear. I felt confident that I could keep up with the class.

When class ended, I helped Merry clean up and put the chairs back against the wall. Andrew helped too.

Our first pottery class had been great. I had learned a lot. It had been easy too! I was sure I could be the perfect pottery student.

Karen's Big Mouth

"How was your pottery class?" asked Hannie at lunch the next day.

Hannie, Nancy, and I were in the cafeteria at school. We were eating hamburgers and french fries.

"It was great!" I said. I dipped a french fry into some ketchup and popped it in my mouth.

"Merry is a wonderful teacher," I said. I spotted Ms. Colman across the cafeteria. I waved. She waved back. "Merry is the second-best teacher I have ever had."

"The class was gigundoly interesting," I continued. "We got to work with clay. Merry explained how firing works, and all about glazes. And you should have seen the recycling tub!"

"Yes," Nancy interrupted me. "We should have." She gave me a pointed look.

Uh-oh. I had a feeling that two of the Musketeers were becoming angry at the third Musketeer again.

"I just asked about your class to be polite," Hannie said. "I did not want to hear so much about it. You do not have to rub our noses in it."

I felt terrible.

"Oh, Hannie, Nancy, I am sorry!" I said. "I did not mean to rub your noses in it. It is just that I am excited about the class. And I really wish you could take it too. Merry should have let you in. But I promise I will not mention it again. Okay?"

Nancy and Hannie exchanged glances.

"Okay," they said.

I could tell they were still upset. I had to say *something* to make them feel better.

"I just want to say one more thing about pottery class." I held up my index finger, to show I really meant *one* more thing.

Hannie and Nancy glanced at each other again. Neither one said anything. I was pretty sure that meant I could go on.

"I was great in the first class," I said. "So far, I have been the perfect pottery student. Merry told me so." (Merry had not actually said that. But she had probably thought it.) "If I keep doing well, I bet Merry will change her mind and let you both in."

"You think so?" Nancy asked.

"Really?" Hannie asked.

"I really think so," I said.

"Wow!" "That would be great!" "I cannot wait!" said Hannie and Nancy. They started planning how they would catch up to the rest of the class, once they were allowed in. They were excited about Merry's class all over again.

Uh-oh. What had I done? Would Merry really let them in the class? She had been pretty definite that she would not. I really had no reason to believe that she would change her mind, no matter how good a student I was.

I had just wanted to make Nancy and Hannie feel better. I had opened my big mouth, and the wrong thing had come out.

I shoved a handful of french fries into my mouth to keep myself from saying anything else. I did not want to cause any more trouble.

Now I was really going to have to be the perfect pottery student. Not only did I have to make Merry love me, I had to make her love me so much that she would let my friends into her class.

The two Musketeers were going to be more upset than ever if they found out they would not be able to take the class.

Turtle, Horse, Eagle

On Tuesday we had our second pottery class. Even though seats were not assigned, everyone sat in the same places they had sat in the first time. So I sat with the same two older girls, and Andrew sat next to me. He had still been copying everything I did, every day, while Merry was at our house. I was getting a little fed up with him.

"Today, class, we are going to do some modeling with the clay," Merry said. She was kneading a lump of clay as she spoke. "I would like each of you to create an animal out of your clay. The animal can be your pet. Or it can be a zoo animal, like an elephant or a seal. It can be a fish, or a bird, or a dinosaur. It can even be an imaginary animal, like a unicorn."

As she spoke, Merry formed the clay with her hands. She made a large ball and flattened it with her hand on the table. Then she attached a small round ball for the head. Smaller, thinner tubes became legs. Merry did not even seem to be watching what she was doing.

"Let your imagination do the work," Merry said. "Capture the life of your animal in the clay."

I was watching Merry's hands closely. Like magic they flattened the four legs into flippers. She pinched the smaller ball and made it pointy, with a little snout. She bent the body at the edges to make a rounded back.

All of a sudden I realized what Merry was making. It was a sea turtle! With a toothpick, Merry etched eyes and a mouth on the head. She drew shell lines on its back.

Merry held up the sea turtle for us to see.

The sea turtle looked almost alive. I could imagine its flippers waving back and forth, gracefully pulling it through the sea. It was beautiful.

Merry plus clay equaled magic.

Soon it was our turn to make something out of clay. I could not decide what animal I should make. I liked cats a lot. Also dogs. And rats. And goldfish. And guinea pigs. And ponies. I even liked hermit crabs. I could hardly name an animal that I did *not* like. (Okay, I was not crazy about slugs.)

The two girls at my table, Isabel Linden and Kathy Mullhouse, were talking about what to make.

"I am going to make a horse," said Isabel.

"Good idea," said Kathy. "I will make an eagle."

Those were good ideas. I especially liked the horse. But a horse's skinny legs might be hard to get right.

Then I remembered that I was trying to be

the perfect student. Good students look up to their teachers and try to be like them. I was sure Merry would be pleased if I made a sea turtle just like hers.

I started shaping my clay the way Merry had. I formed the beginnings of a round body, four short flippers, a head, and a stumpy tail.

After a few minutes, Andrew leaned over and whispered, "Psst! Karen! What are you making?"

"A sea turtle," I whispered back.

"Oh," he said.

I looked at Andrew's clay. It was a big lump with pointy ears and holes for eyes.

"What are making?" I asked. "A really fat cat or dog?"

"No," he said, mushing his clay back into a ball. "I am making a sea turtle too."

He had not been making a sea turtle until I told him I was making one. He was copying again!

Andrew started rolling a clay ball. I went

back to my sea turtle. I sort of hunched over it with my elbow so Andrew could not copy what I was doing.

Pretty soon Merry came around to our table to check on our work.

I held up my sea turtle proudly and said, "See? Just like yours." It was not *quite* as lifelike as Merry's. But it was close.

Merry smiled. "Why, that is very nice, Karen." Then her face became thoughtful. "But you know, you did not *have* to make a sea turtle. Mine was just an example. It was not an assignment."

"Oh, I know," I said. "But your sea turtle was so nice, I wanted to make one just like it!"

"And Andrew," Merry said, turning to him. "What a clever hippopotamus you made."

Andrew looked up at her, surprised. "Thank you," he said.

Hey, wait a minute! I thought. That is a sea turtle, not a hippo! It was so unfair.

Andrew had copied me, which was bad enough. But Merry did not even realize it! I narrowed my eyes at Andrew.

But before I could say anything, Merry moved on. She admired Kathy's eagle. Then she held up Isabel's horse.

"This is very good work, Isabel," Merry said. "I like the way you made the legs so thick. They give your horse real power, and also help it stand up. Well done!"

"Thank you," Isabel said as Merry handed the horse back to her.

Merry had liked Isabel's horse the best. Maybe I had made a mistake in deciding to make a sea turtle.

Maybe I should have made a horse like Isabel's instead.

Andrew Two-Two-Too

The next class was on Thursday. I was more determined than ever to show Merry that I was her best student.

"Today, class, we are going to practice imprinting patterns into clay," said Merry. "But first I will show you how to make a quick and easy bowl."

Merry held up an aluminum pie plate. She took a fist-sized ball of clay and started pressing it into the plate. Soon the inside of the pie plate was lined with clay, like a clay pie crust.

"When the clay dries, it will be in the shape of a shallow bowl," said Merry. "Now I will show you how to put designs into the clay."

On the worktable in front of her Merry had laid out lots of different things — some forks, some bolts and washers and screws, and some marbles. There were bottles, bottle caps, and pencils. There were also some funny-looking metal doodads whose names I did not know.

Merry showed us how to press things into the clay to make patterns. A fork made four lines. The mouth of a bottle made a circle. A washer made two circles. Merry even used the point of a pencil to scratch a line into the clay. It was as if she were drawing with the pencil.

Merry held up her bowl. Though it had taken her only a couple of minutes, Merry's design looked beautiful.

"Now it is your turn to try it," Merry said. She handed out pie plates and lumps of clay.

We all pressed our clay into the plates, to make our shallow bowls. While we were doing that, Merry put some of the pattern-making tools on each table. On my table she put a bottle, a couple of bolts and marbles, two bottle caps, some forks, and some pencils.

"What kind of design are you going to make?" Kathy asked Isabel.

"I am not sure," said Isabel. "I like the pattern the bottle caps make." She reached for a bottle cap.

I was thinking about making my plate look like Merry's. But in the last class, Merry had not seemed to think that was a good idea. She had liked Isabel's horse much better.

I reached for the other bottle cap.

"I think I will use a fork and a pencil too," said Isabel. She picked up one of each.

I did too.

I watched Isabel make her pattern. First she pressed her bottle cap into her clay, to make a zigzaggy circle. Next to the zigzaggy circle, she pressed the fork flat into the clay. Next to that she drew a couple of wavy lines with the pointy end of the pencil, and dotted them with the eraser end. Finally, she repeated the pattern.

I carefully pressed my bottle cap into my clay. Then the fork. Then I drew wavy lines. Then dots. Bottle cap, fork, pencil.

I held up my bowl, taking care not to let Isabel see it. (I was not cheating. This was not a test. But still, I did not want Isabel to see it.) I had completed about half the pattern. My bowl looked great!

I reached for my bottle cap. But I could not find it anywhere.

I looked around my place on the table. I did not see it. Maybe it had rolled off. I ducked down and looked on the floor. It wasn't there.

Then I noticed Andrew. He was pressing it into his clay. And he had a fork and a pencil too! He was copying my pattern.

Andrew was doing everything I did! I felt like I was Karen Two-Two and he was Andrew Two-Two-Too.

"Andrew!" I whispered. "What are you doing?"

"I am making a design," he said. "What are you doing?"

"I am becoming angry with you," I said. "You are being a copycat."

"Am not!"

"Are too!"

"Am not!"

"Are — "

"Karen, is there a problem?" Merry interrupted.

I looked up. Merry was standing next to Isabel. I was about to say that Andrew was copying me. But then I saw that Merry was holding Isabel's bowl.

Perhaps complaining about copying was not the smartest thing to do. After all, I had been copying Isabel. But that was different somehow. (I was not sure exactly how, but it did feel different to me.)

"No, Ms. Perkins," I said. (I called her Ms. Perkins in class, like the rest of the students did.) "No problem."

"Good," said Merry. She turned to Isabel. "This is a wonderful pattern, Isabel. You have a real knack for pottery."

Isabel beamed.

Then Merry stepped around to my side of the table. She looked at my bowl. She looked at me. I smiled. She glanced back at Isabel's bowl. Had she noticed that they were kind of alike?

"Hmm," she said. "Good work, Karen." She looked at Andrew's. "You too, Andrew."

Then she moved on to the next table.

Was that all? She had said Isabel had a "real knack," and yet all I got was "good work."

Something was not right. Merry had liked Isabel's project more than she had liked mine. But they were just the same!

I looked at my bowl, then at Isabel's. Maybe they were not *exactly* the same. Isabel's fork marks were closer to her bottle caps. Her wavy lines were wavier.

It seemed that Isabel was the perfect pottery student. If I could only do everything she did, Merry would think I was perfect too and let Hannie and Nancy into the class.

Next time I would have to be more careful. If I wanted Merry to love my project, I would have to make it *exactly* like Isabel's.

How Does Isabel Do It?

Hannie and Nancy came over to the little house on Saturday afternoon. We played Trapped for a Night in a Haunted House, Stranded for a Year on a Desert Island, and Tiger on the Loose (Midgie was the tiger). All three games were gigundoly fun.

It was a perfect day until Hannie said, "Has Merry said anything about letting us in the pottery class, Karen?"

"Yes," said Nancy, "are we in yet?"

I was about to tell them no when Midgie

darted out from under my bed. "Look out!" I hollered. "Tiger on the loose!"

We all screamed. Midgie ran around in little circles, barking. We screamed some more, then fell over laughing.

Luckily for me, Hannie and Nancy forgot about the pottery class.

At least for the moment.

At the beginning of class on Tuesday, Merry held up a pot. "Here is a pot made by coiling clay," she said. "Today we will coil clay to make a pot, or a bowl, or whatever you wish. Let me show you how."

Merry held up a long, thin rope of clay. "It is easy to do," she said. "Make a snake of clay like this one. Then, starting at one end, coil the clay around itself in a circle. When the circle is big enough to be the base of what you are making, start coiling upward."

As she talked, she showed us what she meant. In no time she had made a simple bowl.

"I did this one quickly, so it is not perfect," Merry said. (It looked pretty good to me.) "It is lopsided, and some of the coils are falling apart. You have to press the coils together gently. You should also gently wet the edges of the coil wherever they touch. That helps them stick together better."

Merry explained some more about coiling. Then she said, "At the end of today's class, we will save our coil projects. Scratch your initials on the bottom of your piece with a toothpick. On Thursday we will work on them some more. Over the weekend they will be fired. And next week we will work on decorating and glazing them."

Wow. The coil projects would be fired and glazed. They would be keepers! I would have to take extra-special care with my coil project. I wanted it to be perfect. I decided to watch Isabel again. I would try to do what she did.

First Isabel rolled her clay out into a long snake. That was easy. I already knew how to do that.

Then she coiled it into a circle, pressing the coils together as she went. She took a small paintbrush, dipped it in water, and wet the edges of the coils wherever they touched. I did the exact same thing.

But then Isabel started coiling up. It looked simple. In one hand she turned the circle of clay she had already made. With the other hand she placed down new clay in a coil.

Somehow I could not do it like she could. My fingers kept getting confused. It was as if I were trying to do everything backward.

My coil was crooked and full of gaps. It looked terrible! Isabel's was perfect.

How did Isabel do it?

I had to squoosh mine up and start all over again. Meanwhile Isabel finished her piece (it was a vase) and scratched her initials on the bottom of it. Then she started on another.

By the time class ended, Isabel had made three perfect coil vases. I had made one vase. And it was not perfect. As I looked at it, its walls fell over. Now it was a bowl. After working hard for a whole class, I had made only one lumpy, stumpy, bumpy *bowl*. Maybe I could give it to Emily Jr. as her food bowl. It looked like the kind of bowl a rat would like.

Boo and bullfrogs!

"I see that some of you have made more than one coil project," said Merry. "I want you to choose the one you like most. We will work on those next class. The others will be recycled."

Isabel chose one of her three perfect vases and carried it to the storage cabinet. Then she put her two rejects on the scrap heap next to the recycling tub.

Class was over.

As usual, Andrew and I stayed behind to help Merry tidy up.

I helped Andrew move chairs for awhile. Then I wandered over to the recycling tub. I wanted to get a closer look at Isabel's vases. How *had* she done it?

I picked up the one on top.

"Why, Karen," said Merry.

I spun around. I was holding Isabel's vase in front of me.

"Why, Karen," Merry repeated. "Your vase is lovely. You should put it in the storage cabinet with the others. You will want to work on it again on Thursday."

The Big Switch

"**Y**ou do not understand," I said. "This is not my — "

"Not your best work?" Merry said. "Well, you only had one class period to work on it. You can work on it again on Thursday. It would be a shame to put it in the recycling tub."

She gently led me toward the storage cabinet.

"But — but," I stammered. My mind was whirling.

"That is a *terrific* first try, Karen," Merry

said, smiling. "You really have a feel for pottery. I knew you could do it. Now, put your vase in the cupboard while I run outside to get another garbage bag."

She left me standing at the storage cabinet, holding Isabel's vase. I did not know what to do. I had tried to explain that it was not mine, but Merry had not let me. She wanted me to save the vase. She was happy with *this* vase.

I looked down at it. I thought of my rat bowl.

I knew I should rush back to the recycling tub and toss the vase in. But Merry had said it would be a shame to recycle the vase.

Should I save it instead? I thought and thought.

Isabel was going to throw it out anyway. She did not want it anymore. If I saved it from the recycling tub, it was not really stealing, was it?

And Merry *did* say it was lovely. She said I had a feel for pottery.

I opened the storage cabinet and looked

at my bowl. It was saggy, baggy, and draggy.

I looked at the vase in my hands. It was perfect.

Merry would not have said my rat bowl was lovely. She would not have thought I had a feel for pottery. She would have thought I was too young for this class. And she would have thought she had made a mistake letting Andrew and me take her class.

My face burning, I turned Isabel's vase over. Her initials were scratched in the bottom:

I L

Quickly, before I could change my mind, I grabbed a pencil out of a cup in the storage cabinet. I changed the initials on the bottom of the vase to:

KB

Then I placed my new vase on the shelf and snatched up my bowl. As I rushed it to the recycling tub, I felt as if I were in a dream. I could not believe I was actually doing this.

I tossed my bowl into the tub. Bubble, bubble, down it sank. I felt terrible. But the deed was done.

I looked around. Had anyone seen what I had done?

Andrew was busy shoving chairs around. Merry had not come back yet.

I had pulled the Big Switch. And I had gotten away with it.

Karen Is Doomed

There was no way I was going to get away with it. I realized that the next day.

Switching projects was wrong. I had known it was wrong when I did it. It was dishonest. Only a meanie-mo would do it.

And I was going to get caught. On Thursday Isabel would recognize her vase. She would accuse me of stealing. The truth would come out. Everyone would know what I had done.

Merry would hate me. Even Andrew

would lose respect for me. (He would probably stop copying me, though.)

I was doomed.

"I am doomed," I moaned on the bus to school.

"I am doomed," I moaned before class.

"I am doomed," I moaned in the lunch line.

"Why do you keep saying you are doomed, Karen?" asked Hannie.

"Do you have some horrible disease?" asked Nancy, looking worried.

"I wish," I said. "But I am not that lucky. I am dooooomed."

Hannie and Nancy drew circles in the air next to their heads. They thought I was going crazy.

I wanted to tell them why I was doomed — but I was too ashamed. I did not want my best friends to know about the terrible thing I had done.

And besides, I did not want to bring up the subject of Merry's class. Hannie and Nancy were still wondering when they would be allowed to join. I did not want them to know I had ruined their chances.

They did not know how lucky they were not to be taking pottery class. It was nothing but Trouble with a capital *T*.

"I am home," I said sadly after school.

"Karen!" Andrew came running to greet me. "Guess what! Merry and I had so much fun this afternoon. First we made . . ."

Usually I am very happy to see Andrew when I get home from school. But today had been a terrible day. I did not want to see anyone or talk to anyone.

Andrew said, ". . . and then we went outside to look for tulips, and — "

"Andrew," I said, interrupting him. "I am sorry, but I am in a bad mood."

Andrew's face grew serious. "Oh, me too," he said.

"I just want to be alone."

"Me too."

I started to walk upstairs to my room. Andrew followed me.

I stopped and turned to face him. "Andrew, did you understand what I said?" I asked. "I do not want to see anyone right now."

"Me too!" Andrew said.

I marched down the hall. I opened the door to my room. I started to close it, but Andrew was in the way.

"Andrew, stop following me!" I said.

"I am not following you!"

"Yes you are! You are a copycat and a pest."

"Am not!"

"Are too! Copycat! Pest!" I yelled.

Andrew burst into tears and ran down the hall to his room.

Now I had done it.

I heard Merry in the hall. I remembered I wanted to be on my best behavior. I remembered I wanted to be the most wonderful child in the world. I remembered I wanted to make Merry love us. Now I had blown it.

Merry came into my room and shut the door behind her. That is never a good sign.

"I could not help overhearing your fight with Andrew," Merry said. "What was all the yelling about?" She smiled. I could not smile back.

"You know, Karen," Merry went on, "Andrew is not trying to bother you. He is only four."

"Going on five," I reminded her.

"Right, going on five," Merry said. "Sometimes little kids like Andrew do not realize that they can be annoying. He is not following you around and copying you to make you mad. He is doing it because he looks up to you. He wants to be like you."

I had not thought of that.

"Try to keep that in mind the next time he gets on your nerves," said Merry. "Okay?"

I nodded. "Okay."

"Now I am going to talk to Andrew," said Merry. She opened the door to leave, then paused in the doorway. "I think your brother is a very special child, you know. And I think you are too."

Merry started to walk down the hall to Andrew's room.

"Merry?" I called after her.

She turned. "Yes?"

I smiled. "Thanks. I think you are special too."

Karen Is Saved

After Merry was so nice to me, I felt worse than ever. How could I tell her that I had switched projects with another student?

I could not.

But it did not matter. I knew that as soon as Isabel Linden saw "my" vase, she would recognize it as hers. I would be caught.

Before class on Thursday I sat stiffly at my table, waiting for Isabel to arrive. It was pure torture. All the other students were at their seats. Isabel was late.

Then Merry announced, "Isabel Linden's

mother just called. Isabel has a cold and will not be coming to today's class."

I almost fell out of my chair. Isabel was sick. Hooray! I knew it was not very nice to be glad that Isabel was sick, but I could not help it. I was saved, saved, saved!

At least for now.

I raced to the storage cabinet to retrieve my vase.

Just in case Isabel recovered soon, I would have to disguise the vase. If I decorated it enough, Isabel might not recognize it.

I sat happily at my table, scratching a tiny triangle pattern into the rim of the vase. I hummed a little tune ("Everything's Coming Up Roses") as I worked.

"Stop it," said Andrew.

I turned to him. He was making a family of clay snakes. He had given up on making a coil project.

"Stop what?" I asked.

"That humming," he said. "It is bothering me."

Andrew was still mad at me for yelling at him the day before.

I did not want to tease him on purpose, so I stopped humming. I worked on my vase some more.

"Stop it!" Andrew said.

"Stop what?"

"Stop that humming! You were doing it again."

"Was not!"

"Were too!"

I turned to Kathy Mullhouse, on the other side of the table.

"Was I humming?" I asked her.

"Yes, you were," she said. "And it *is* a little annoying."

Hmph. I do not know why Andrew and Kathy thought my humming was annoying. I am a good hummer.

"I will not do it again," I said to Kathy. Then to Andrew I said, "Happy now?"

He nodded but did not say anything. He went back to rolling out snake children.

When Andrew is mad, he sure can be frosty.

Oh, well. At least he was not following me around and copying me anymore. And he would get over being mad at me someday.

I hoped.

By the time class was over, I had decorated the rim of the vase with triangles. And I had added a pattern of squiggly lines around the center. Isabel would never know the vase had been hers.

My vase was ready to be fired over the weekend.

What Friends Are For

"Mission control to Alpha Seven," said Hannie. It was Saturday afternoon. She was sitting on the rug in my room. "Come in, Alpha Seven."

"Alpha Seven here," said Nancy into her pretend wrist-communicator. She was sitting on my bed. "I was forced to crash-land on the planet Zornax. Aliens have the ship surrounded."

"Rrrawk!" I roared. I sprang up from the floor and leaped on Nancy. I started tickling her.

"Mayday, mayday!" Nancy yelled, trying not to giggle. "Alien attacking!"

"Firing Earth-to-Zornax missile!" Hannie shouted. She jumped on top of Nancy and me.

We wrestled around on the bed, shrieking and giggling. Space Explorers is a gigundoly fun game, but it never lasts very long. Someone always winds up death-ray-blasted.

"Zzzap!" Nancy fired her finger into my stomach. "Got you, you hideous nine-armed Zornaxian freak!"

"Arrrgh!" I clutched my stomach and rolled off the bed. I writhed on the floor, thrashing all nine of my tentacles. At last I lay still. (I do great death scenes. I might be an actress when I grow up.)

"That was fun," said Hannie. "Do you want to play again? I will be the alien this time."

"Or we could call Midgie," said Nancy. "Maybe she would be up for a game of Tiger on the Loose."

"Okay." I leaped off the floor.

We ran through the house, calling for Midgie. For some reason we could not find her. (It was almost as if she were hiding from us. We could not find Rocky either.)

Finally we met back in my room.

"I guess the tiger is not on the loose," I said.

"I guess not," said Nancy.

"So what do you want to do now?" Hannie asked.

"We could play School," I suggested.

"That is a good game," said Nancy. "Who wants to be the teacher?"

"I will," I said. "I will be Merry."

Oops. As soon as I said it, I knew it was a mistake.

"I mean Ms. Colman," I said quickly. "I will be Ms. Colman."

"No, you can be Merry," said Hannie. "We can play Pottery Class. It will be good practice for when Nancy and I are actually in the class."

"Yes," said Nancy. "And by the way,

Karen, when *are* we going to be allowed in the class?"

"Um . . ." I said. "I have some good news and some bad news."

"Oh, no!" said Hannie. "Not this again! You had better have some good news this time, Karen."

"I do, sort of," I said. "But first the bad news. The bad news is I really do not think Merry is ever going to let you into the pottery class."

"I had a feeling that was going to be the bad news," said Hannie.

Nancy nodded. "I had that feeling too. So what is the good news?"

"The good news is you would not want to be in the class anyway," I said. "You should be glad you are not taking Merry's class."

"What?" said Nancy.

"Why?" asked Hannie. "Is Merry a bad teacher?"

"No, no," I said. "Merry is a wonderful teacher."

"Then why should we be glad we are not in her class?" Nancy asked.

I had to tell them about the Big Switch. They were my best friends. They would understand.

So I did. It all came out. I told how I had tried to copy Isabel's vase. How I had switched hers for my own. How I had changed her initials. (Hannie and Nancy gasped at that.) How I had decorated it during the last class, when Isabel was absent.

"What should I do?" I wailed. "My vase is getting fired today. It is too late to put it back in the recycling tub. What will happen when Isabel figures out what happened?"

Hannie and Nancy stared at me. Their eyes were wide.

"What's wrong?" I asked.

"We cannot believe you," said Hannie.

"I would never have been able to steal someone else's vase," Nancy said.

"What should I do now?" I asked.

"Well, you could confess," said Nancy.

"Maybe Merry would not be too mad at you."

"But she probably would be," said Hannie.

I agreed with Hannie.

"You say you decorated the vase?" Hannie asked. "It does not look the way it did when Isabel put it on the recycle pile?"

"Right," I said.

"Then you are in too deep to back out now," said Hannie. "You just have to hope for the best. Maybe Isabel will not come back. Even if she does, she will never in a million years recognize her old thrown-out vase that has new decorations on it."

Nancy nodded. "You do not seem to have much choice, Karen."

I sat silently for a minute. Finally I said, "You are right. I will just have to hope I get away with it."

Hannie and Nancy nodded.

"And you were right too, Karen," said Hannie.

"Right about what?" I asked.

"Right when you said you had some good news. I certainly am glad I am not in Merry's pottery class. I could not take the excitement."

I laughed. I was lucky to have friends like the two Musketeers.

Isabel Returns

By Tuesday afternoon I had decided I was going to get away with it. Maybe Isabel would not be back in class yet. Even if she were, she would never recognize her old vase.

I might even win some sort of prize, for best coil project.

Andrew and I hurried into the classroom with Merry. Who should I see at our table but — Isabel Linden!

"Isabel!" I said. "You are back!"

"Yes," she replied. "I just had a cold. I

came to class early today to work on my vase." She held up her unfired vase from last week. "I need to catch up with the rest of the class."

Uh-oh, I thought.

Pretty soon Merry started class.

"Here are the coil projects that were fired over the weekend," said Merry. She brought out a tray full of pottery. Instead of a dark wettish gray, the fired pieces now were a lighter, sandier color.

"You have done some excellent work," Merry said. She started walking around the room. "Jessica Orvieto's bowl is very nice." She handed a bowl to one of the students. "Stewart King's pencil holder is well made." She handed the pencil holder to a boy. She passed out several more pieces.

Merry headed toward me. "Karen Brewer's vase is quite nice too," she said. She gave me the vase and whispered, "Good work, Karen."

"Thank you," I whispered back.

Then I glanced across the table at Isabel.

She was staring hard at the vase in my hand.

Suddenly I felt the back of my neck go warm. I could feel myself blushing.

Isabel's eyes met mine.

Her eyes went back down to the vase.

Then up to my eyes again.

Back to the vase.

Up to my eyes.

"May I see your vase, please, Karen?" Isabel asked sweetly. She held out her hand.

How could I refuse?

"Uh, sure," I said. I reached across the table and placed the vase in her outstretched hand.

"Thank you," she said.

I watched Isabel closely as she examined the vase. Turned it over to check the initials on the bottom. Held it this way and that. Turned it over again.

She set the vase on the table in front of her.

At last she spoke. "I made this," she said. "Where did you get it?"

My heart started thumping hard. My mouth went dry. I could hardly get a word out in reply.

"It is not yours," I croaked.

"Yes, it is," Isabel said. Her voice was louder. "I made it. Somehow you stole it." I wanted to say *Indoor voice, Isabel.*

"I did not steal anything," I said.

"Did too!" Isabel practically shouted.

The classroom fell silent.

"What is all this commotion about?" Merry asked.

Isabel held up the vase. "This vase is not Karen's. I made it. I know I did."

"That is the vase I have been working on all week," I said. (That was true.) "My initials are on the bottom." (That was true too. I did not want to lie to Merry.)

"Maybe so," said Isabel. "But I made it. And I can prove it!"

Caught in a Coil

"You cannot prove anything," I said to Isabel.

My face was burning. Did I look as guilty as I felt? As long as Isabel could not prove the vase was hers, I would be okay.

I hoped hard that Isabel would not be able to prove a thing.

"I can too," said Isabel.

"How?" asked Merry. (Merry was standing next to me, but I did not look up at her. I was too ashamed to meet her eye.)

"Yeah, Isabel," I said. I tried to sound confident. "How?"

"Just wait," said Isabel. She started rolling out some fresh clay into a long snake.

"Here," she said, finishing the clay snake. She handed it across the table to me.

"What do you want me to do with this?" I asked.

"Coil it up. Make another vase," said Isabel.

She did not think I could make a coil vase at all. Well, I would show her. I *had* made a coil vase. Maybe it had collapsed and become a coil bowl — but still, I knew how to do it. I had not been going to pottery class for nothing.

I started coiling up the clay. I did the base, then started building the sides.

But the sides started to droop and drop.

"This is not fair," I said. "I am very nervous. I am not taking my time."

The vase fell in on itself. Another bowl for Emily Jr. I placed it on the table in front of me.

"Of course I cannot make a good vase right now," I said. "If I were not in such a hurry, I could do much better."

"Maybe so," said Isabel. She put the fired vase (which she had been holding all this time) next to my droopy fresh vase. "But that is not the point."

"What is the point, Isabel?" Merry asked.

"Look at *my* vase" — Isabel stressed the "my" — "and look at hers." She picked them up and held them in front of Merry.

"Yes?" said Merry.

"Look at the way her coil runs," said Isabel. "Starting from the center, the clay coils out clockwise. See? I noticed last week that *everybody's* coils go clockwise."

"So?" I butted in. "What has that got to with — "

"Let Isabel finish, Karen," said Merry.

"I was about to say, everybody's coils go clockwise — except mine," said Isabel. She handed the fired vase to Merry. "See? The coils run the opposite direction. *All* of *my* coils go counterclockwise."

94

Isabel handed Merry her other vase — the unfired one that she had saved from last week.

"My coil is different because I am left-handed," said Isabel. "Everybody else in the class is right-handed. Including Karen."

Merry looked at the three vases for a long, long time. Then, without saying anything, she walked around the room, looking at other coil projects. She was checking to see whether the coils ran clockwise or counterclockwise. I wanted the floor to open up and swallow me, vase and all.

Finally she made her way back to my table.

"Karen?" Merry asked. "Isabel has a point. I am going to ask you one time, and one time only: Did Isabel make the vase that you have been working on?"

I could have lied. If I had lied, Isabel would have been furious. But that was not what worried me. Merry would probably have taken my word for it. She was my nanny, after all. And she had said she would not ask me about it again.

So all I had to do was lie.

But I would never be able to look Merry in the face ever again.

"Merry, I — " I started to say. I couldn't finish. I burst into tears. Between sobs, I finally managed to say, "Isabel is right! The vase was hers."

Karen's Confession

The next hour was the longest sixty minutes of my life. I sat at a table in the back of the classroom, away from the other students. I was in disgrace.

Andrew sat with me. He is a loyal little brother, even if he is sometimes a copycat. I think he could not believe what I had done.

Every now and then a student would turn around and look at me, then whisper something to a friend. I could just imagine what they were saying.

Finally class ended.

Merry asked Andrew to help put the chairs back against the wall. When he had gone, Merry said to me, "Karen, what happened? Why did you take a project that did not belong to you?"

I had been thinking about that very question. And I had had one very long hour to come up with an answer. So I explained it to Merry as best I could.

"I do not know," I said. "It started off as a mistake. Isabel had put the vase on the recycle pile, and I had picked it up to look at it. I wanted to see how she did it. Her work was so much better than mine. Then you saw me with it and thought it was mine. You told me how much you liked it. I did not want to disappoint you. I wanted you to think I was good at pottery. And Isabel was getting rid of it anyway. The next thing I knew, I was pretending it *was* mine. I changed the initials on the bottom, put it on the shelf, and threw away the vase I had made, which was really a bowl. You know the rest of the story.

"Oh, Merry, I am so, so sorry!" I exclaimed. My eyes started to get teary again, and I sniffled. "You must think I am the worst kid in the whole world. And I just wanted to be your best student so you would like me as much as I like you!"

"Oh, Karen," said Merry. She put her arm around me and I buried my face in her shoulder.

"You know, Karen, I think I may be partly to blame here too," said Merry.

"You?" I asked. "How?"

"I should have been more sensitive to your feelings," Merry said. "Do you remember last week, when you and Andrew had a fight about copying?"

"Uh-huh." I nodded. I sniffled and hiccuped.

"Afterward, I had a talk with Andrew," Merry said. "He told me he missed having your mom around all day. He was feeling lonely and sad. Getting used to a new nanny was not easy for Andrew. I think that

is why he was following you around and copying you — he wanted to stay extra close to you."

"Oh," I said. Poor Andrew. Now I felt even worse about yelling at him. "But what has that got to do with Isabel's vase?"

"You are such a grown-up young lady, I figured you would have no trouble adjusting to me," said Merry. "I see now that having a new nanny was not so easy for you either. You were worried about how you and I would get along. Am I right?"

"I guess so," I said. "When you said Hannie and Nancy could not take the pottery class, I wondered if you really liked me."

Merry smiled. "Of course I like you," she said. "I simply did not want to bend the rules to let anyone else in the class. Anyway, I think you copied my turtle on the first day of class because you were worried."

"I wanted you to think I was the perfect pottery student," I explained.

"And that's why you started copying Isabel too — to impress me. And why you ended up claiming her vase as your own."

"I am so, so sorry, Merry," I said again. (I have noticed that once you decide to apologize, you cannot apologize too much.)

"I forgive you, Karen," said Merry. She gave me a nice warm hug. "There was no need to impress me. I think you and Andrew are the best kids in the whole world."

"Really?" I asked, feeling a thousand times happier. "Because I think you are the best nanny in the whole world."

We hugged again.

Setting Things Right

"Whew!" I said. "Am I glad that is over."

"Karen," said Merry. "It is not quite over yet. There are some things you need to do to set things right."

"Oh, yeah," I said. "Like apologize to Andrew for yelling at him last week?"

"That would be a good place to start," said Merry.

"I owe Isabel an apology too."

Merry nodded.

"That is going to be a tough one," I said.

Merry nodded again.

"But I will do it. And I guess I should be punished for switching the vases and lying, right?"

"Well, the thought had occurred to me," Merry said.

I looked around the room. Andrew was dragging the last couple of chairs to the wall.

"How about if I move all the chairs by myself from now on, before and after class?" I suggested.

"Actually, I think Andrew enjoys moving the chairs," said Merry. "So if he wants to help you, you must let him. Otherwise it is your chore. Also, I would like you to sponge down all the tables after class."

"That is fair," I said. Then I swallowed hard. The last thing I would have to do would be the hardest of all, by far. "And I will have to tell Mommy and Seth what happened. Right?"

Merry smiled. "I am afraid you will," she said. "But here is the deal: You must tell them you got in trouble in pottery class. But speaking as your nanny, I do not think you need to go into too much detail about what happened. It is really between you and your pottery teacher. And speaking as your pottery teacher, I think we have worked it out between us in a satisfactory way."

"Thank you, Merry," I said. I gave her another hug.

Andrew ran to us then.

"Hey," he said. "Do I get a hug?"

"Yes!" I shouted. I pulled him into our hug. "Group hug! Group hug!"

Merry and Andrew and I laughed and laughed and laughed.

And One for All!

"Rain, rain, go away, come again another day," I sang.

I was sitting in the car with Hannie, Nancy, and Andrew. Merry was driving us to the community center. I listened to the *whick-whick, whick-whick* of the windshield wipers. I love being warm and snug in the car when it is raining outside.

March had come in like a lion. Not going out like a lamb, though. More like a lion cub.

Mommy and Seth were not pleased to

learn that I had been a pottery-class trouble-maker. But they did not ask for details (I had a feeling Merry had asked them not to). They said that if Merry was satisfied that I had been punished, then they would not punish me further. Merry told them that it was all taken care of.

Andrew and I were friends again. I had told him I was sorry for calling him a copycat. He had told me he was sorry for *being* a copycat. We agreed to be nicer to each other in the future.

I apologized to Isabel Linden too. She was not as nice about my apology as Andrew had been. She said, "Okay," but I could tell she did not mean it.

If I were Isabel, I would not forgive me very quickly either.

The last couple of pottery classes were really fun. I had to start all over on a new coil project. (This time I made a pencil holder. It was a little easier than a vase.) After it was fired, I glazed it, and then the glaze was fired.

The glaze turned out sort of shiny blue-green with little brownish spots showing through. (It looked prettier than it sounds.) I loved the way it looked.

I gave the pencil holder to Merry. I thought she deserved it.

When I presented it to her, Merry said, "Why, thank you, Karen. That is a very sweet gesture. And now I have a place to keep all my pencils."

I grinned and said, "I really learned a lot in your class, Merry, and not just about pottery."

"I am glad you did, Karen. I learned a lot too. I know a class has gone well when both the students and the teacher learned something in it."

"You are probably right," I said. I never knew that teachers could learn from students too.

On the last day of class, we had a show of our work. My pencil holder was in it. Andrew's snake family was in it. But the star of the show was Isabel's vase. (Not the one I had been working on. I never found out what Isabel did with that one.) Everybody oohed and ahhed over Isabel's vase.

On the whole, I would say pottery class was fun. But I was very glad it was over.

Still, there was one more pottery lesson to come.

"Are you ready, Musketeers?" I asked.

"Yes! Ready!" shouted Hannie and Nancy.

"Ready!" shouted Andrew. (When he is with us, sometimes we let him be a fourth Musketeer.)

Merry was taking us to the community center for a special private lesson. She even promised to show us how to use the pottery wheel.

The wheel is a big platter that spins around. You put a lump of wet clay in the center. As the clay spins, you shape it with your hands to make bowls and cups and things. When Merry does it, the clay looks alive. Bowls appear like magic.

Merry said using the wheel is difficult at first, but becomes much easier with practice.

I could not wait to use it.

"Okay, Musketeers," I said. Merry pulled into the parking lot of the community center. "Here we are!"

I was excited about using the wheel. I was excited about having the best nanny ever. I was excited about being with the Musketeers. I could not stop myself. I just had to shout out our motto.

"All for one — " I hollered.

And you can guess what Hannie, Nancy, and Andrew shouted back.

L. GODWIN

About the Author

ANN M. MARTIN lives in New York City and loves animals, especially cats. She has two cats of her own, Gussie and Woody.

Other books by Ann M. Martin that you might enjoy are *Stage Fright*; *Me and Katie (the Pest)*; and the books in *The Baby-sitters Club* series.

Ann likes ice cream and *I Love Lucy*. And she has her own little sister, whose name is Jane.

Little Sister

Don't miss #108

KAREN'S FIELD DAY

"Gym is almost over," said Mrs. Mackey when she had everyone's attention. "Before we go inside, I want to explain about our upcoming Field Day."

"Yea!" we all shouted. Everyone loves Field Day. I forgot all about basketball.

"There will be eight events," Mrs. Mackey said. She ticked them off on her fingers. "Fifty-meter sprint. Four-hundred meter run. Four-person relay race. Standing long jump. Sack race. Wheelbarrow race. Three-legged race. Water-balloon toss."

Everyone started talking all at once about the Field Day events. We could not help it. It was too exciting.

Tweet! "Ten points will be given for finishing first in any event. Five points for second. And two points for third," said Mrs. Mackey. "Whoever has the most points in each grade at the end of the day will win a gift certificate to Phil's Sporting Goods."

Little Sister

by Ann M. Martin
author of The Baby-sitters Club®

More Titles... ➡

Available wherever you buy books, or use this order form.

Scholastic Inc., P.O. Box 7502, Jefferson City, MO 65102

Please send me the books I have checked above. I am enclosing $_____
(please add $2.00 to cover shipping and handling). Send check or money order – no cash or C.O.Ds please.

Name_____ Birthdate_____

Address_____

City_____ State/Zip_____

Please allow four to six weeks for delivery. Offer good in U.S.A. only. Sorry, mail orders are not available to residents of Canada. Prices subject to change.   BSLS998

LITTLE  APPLE®

Here are some of our favorite Little Apples.

Once you take a bite out of a Little Apple book—you'll want to read more!

Books for Kids with BIG Appetites!

❑ NA45899-X **Amber Brown Is Not a Crayon**
  Paula Danziger **$2.99**

❑ NA42833-0 **Catwings** Ursula K. LeGuin **$3.50**

❑ NA42832-2 **Catwings Return** Ursula K. LeGuin **$3.50**

❑ NA41821-1 **Class Clown** Johanna Hurwitz **$3.50**

❑ NA42400-9 **Five True Horse Stories** Margaret Davidson **$3.50**

❑ NA42401-7 **Five True Dog Stories** Margaret Davidson **$3.50**

❑ NA43868-9 **The Haunting of Grade Three**
  Grace Maccarone **$3.50**

❑ NA40966-2 **Rent a Third Grader** B.B. Hiller **$3.50**

❑ NA41944-7 **The Return of the Third Grade Ghost Hunters**
  Grace Maccarone **$2.99**

❑ NA47463-4 **Second Grade Friends** Miriam Cohen **$3.50**

❑ NA45729-2 **Striped Ice Cream** Joan M. Lexau **$3.50**